READING CHAMPION

Sid's Stick

by **Katie Dale** and **Charlie Alder**

W

FRANKLIN WATTS
LONDON • SYDNEY

Sid likes to play with sticks.

Where is Sid's stick?

Here it is.

Get the stick, Sid.

No, that is a rake.

Look out, Sid!

Where is Sid's stick?

Here it is.

Get the stick, Sid.

No, that is a ladder.

Look out, Sid!

Where is Sid's stick?

Here it is.

Get the stick, Sid.

No, that is a cat.

Look out, Sid!

Yes!

Here is Sid's stick.

Get the stick, Sid.

Get the stick!

Sid likes to play.

The brown dog likes to play.

Get the stick.

Story trail

Start

Start at the beginning of the story trail. Ask your child to retell the story in their own words, pointing to each picture in turn to recall the sequence of events.

Independent Reading

This series is designed to provide an opportunity for your child to read on their own. These notes are written for you to help your child choose a book and to read it independently.

In school, your child's teacher will often be using reading books which have been banded to support the process of learning to read. Use the book band colour your child is reading in school to help you make a good choice. *Sid's Stick* is a good choice for children reading at Yellow Band in their classroom to read independently.

The aim of independent reading is to read this book with ease, so that your child enjoys the story and relates it to their own experiences.

About the book

Sid the dog is desperate to find his stick, but he keeps picking up the wrong thing. Then he finds another dog at the end of his stick! The two of them are soon great friends.

Before reading

Help your child to learn how to make good choices by asking: "Why did you choose this book? Why do you think you will enjoy it?" Look at the cover together and ask: "What do you think the story will be about?" Support your child to think of what they already know about the story context. Read the title aloud and ask: "Do you think Sid is the dog or the boy? Why do you think that?" Remind your child that they can try to sound out the letters to make a word if they get stuck.

Decide together whether your child will read the story independently or read it aloud to you. When books are short, as at Yellow Band, your child may wish to do both!

During reading

If reading aloud, support your child if they hesitate or ask for help by telling the word. Remind your child of what they know and what they can do independently.

If reading to themselves, remind your child that they can come and ask for your help if stuck.

After reading

Support comprehension by asking your child to tell you about the story. Help your child think about the messages in the book that go beyond the story and ask: "Do you think Sid will have more fun at the end of the story? Why / why not?"

Give your child a chance to respond to the story: "Did you have a favourite part? Do you think it is more fun to play on your own or share a game with a friend?"

Use the story trail to encourage your child to retell the story in the right sequence, in their own words.

Extending learning

Help your child understand the story structure by using the same sentence patterns and adding some new elements. "Let's make up a new story about a cat called Kit and something she likes to play with. 'Kit likes to play with string. Where is Kit's string? Here it is! Get the string, Kit. No, that is a worm. Look out, Kit!' Now you try. What will Kit mistake for her string in your story?"

Your child's teacher will be talking about punctuation at Yellow Band. On a few of the pages, check your child can recognise capital letters, question marks, exclamation marks and full stops by asking them to point these out.

Franklin Watts
First published in Great Britain in 2017
by The Watts Publishing Group

Series Editors: Jackie Hamley and Melanie Palmer
Series Advisors: Dr Sue Bodman and Glen Franklin
Series Designer: Peter Scoulding

A CIP catalogue record for this book is
available from the British Library.

ISBN 978 1 4451 5471 8 (hbk)
ISBN 978 1 4451 5472 5 (pbk)
ISBN 978 1 4451 6080 1 (library ebook)

Printed in China

Franklin Watts
An imprint of
Hachette Children's Group
Part of The Watts Publishing Group
Carmelite House
50 Victoria Embankment
London EC4Y 0DZ

An Hachette UK Company
www.hachette.co.uk

www.franklinwatts.co.uk

FSC
www.fsc.org
MIX
Paper from
responsible sources
FSC® C104740